For John S. and Ari B.

—K.C.

For Aldo

—N.M.

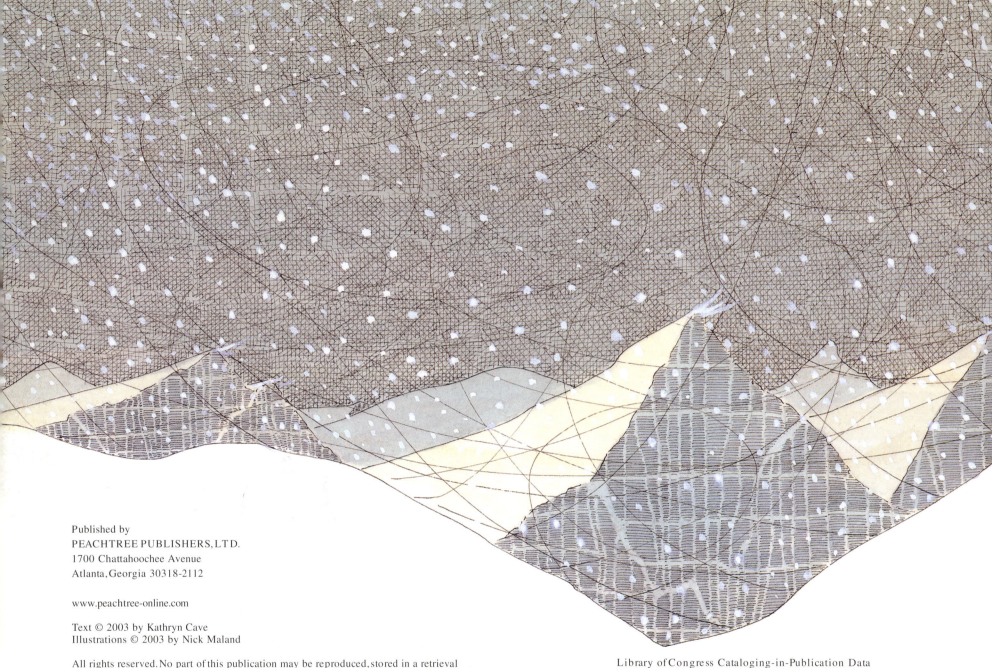

Published by
PEACHTREE PUBLISHERS, LTD.
1700 Chattahoochee Avenue
Atlanta, Georgia 30318-2112

www.peachtree-online.com

Text © 2003 by Kathryn Cave
Illustrations © 2003 by Nick Maland

First published in Great Britain in 2003 by Hodder Children's Books

Manufactured in Hong Kong

10 9 8 7 6 5 4 3 2 1
First Edition

Library of Congress Cataloging-in-Publication Data

Cave, Kathryn.
 You've got dragons / written by Kathryn Cave ; illustrated by Nick Maland.-- 1st ed.
   p. cm.
Summary: A young boy discovers that he has worries and fears that appear to him as dragons and shares what he learns about living with them.
 ISBN 1-56145-284-X
 [1. Dragons--Fiction. 2. Fear--Fiction.] I. Maland, Nick, ill. II. Title.
 PZ7.C29114 Yo 2003
 [E]--dc21
                                                2002015655

YOU'VE GOT DRAGONS

Written by **Kathryn Cave**

Illustrated by **Nick Maland**

PEACHTREE

ATLANTA

Dragons show up when you least expect them.
You turn around...

...and there they are.

Am I dreaming? you think.
And you pinch yourself, hard.

But you're not.

Your heart thuds and your knees
wobble and your hands shake and
your head whirls and you feel
hot and cold and you can't breathe
and your tummy hurts and you can't
believe it's really happening to you.

But it is. It really is.

You've got dragons.

You've never had dragons before.
You're not sure what to do.

You say to yourself:

Why me? Why am I the one to get dragons?
Was it something I did? I've been bad sometimes.
But not THAT bad. And mostly I'm good.
I've never been bad enough to deserve THIS.

You're right. Nobody deserves dragons.
YOU certainly don't.
You didn't get them by being bad.

All these people have
dragons, and they're
REALLY, REALLY good.

Dragons are scary.
You try to pretend yours
isn't there.

But it IS.

Pretending a dragon isn't there is
VERY hard work.

You keep checking to make sure it's
still there. You have to check in all
sorts of places. Sometimes you think
it really ISN'T there.

But it IS.

Pretending a huge, great, ENORMOUS dragon isn't there is exhausting.
    So sooner or later you stop pretending.

Then you say:

OK, it's there—but it isn't a dragon.

It's a mouse. Who's scared of a mouse?

But that's some mouse!

Look at its shadow.

That mouse looks just like a dragon.

**Deep down, you KNOW it's a dragon.
You're still scared.**

Now that you've got dragons, you can't get away from them.
They pop up all the time:

when you wake up, when you brush your teeth,

when you go to school, when you eat lunch,

when you walk home,

when you play games,

when you turn on the television, when you go to bed,

when you turn off the light.

ESPECIALLY when you turn off the light.

So sometimes you leave it on.

You don't want to think about dragons, but you do—all the time.

How do you spell CAT?
d-r-a-g-o-n

Big, bigger, ...?
dragon-sized.

Who are you?
A dragon.

$2 + 2 = ?$
4 dragons
$2 \times 6 = ?$
12 dragons

You make silly mistakes because of the dragons.

What's this?

A dragon.

You're worried that people won't understand. If you tried to explain, they might think you were weird. So you don't say anything.

Dragons make everything complicated.

Sometimes people try to talk to you about them when you don't want to talk.

So, how's the old dragon today, hmmm?

Or sometimes when you DO want to talk, they're too busy or they don't want to listen or they don't understand.
Or THEY want to do all the talking.

Let me tell you about MY dragon...

Sometimes you feel like you're burning up inside. You want to shout at the dragon: *GO AWAY!* You'd like to stomp on it and kill it.

But you'd need very big shoes.

It seems so much bigger than you.

Sometimes you get cold and shivery and you don't want to be alone.

Soon you are the world's greatest expert on having dragons.

By popular demand: # Ben's Advice Column

Dear Ben,
I want to run away from
my dragon. What kind of
training should I do? (I am
six years old.) Do I need
special shoes? If so, please
tell me where I can get pink
ones.
Sincerely,
Sophie

Dear Sophie,
Special shoes and
training won't help.
Take it from me,
dragons are too fast
to run away from.
Yours,
Ben

Dear Ben,
I have been trying to
hide from my dragons
for forty-three years,
eight months, and four days.
Can you recommend a
foolproof hiding place?
Hopefully,
Dad

Dear Dad,
Try under the stairs.
It's more comfy than under
the bed. (I always wondered
what you were doing there.)
Your loving son,
Ben
P.S. Say "Hi" to your dragons when
they find you. They will.

Dear Ben,
I got dragons last month when
we moved to our new house. Now my
tummy hurts every morning. Is this
normal? I also have purple spots on
my tongue. What do you suggest I do?
Anxiously,
Dave

Dear Dave,
In answer to your letter:
1. *Yes.*
2. *Stop chewing on your markers.*
It makes your teeth
purple too.
Your friend,
Ben

BEN'S TOP TIPS FOR WHAT TO DO WHEN YOU'VE GOT DRAGONS

1. Give your dragon your full attention at least once a day. Dragons get bigger when they are ignored.

Greetings, honorable dragon.
Greetings, honorable Ben.

2. Really get to know your dragon. Give it a name. What sort of dragon is it? Look at it hard, then draw a picture of it.

THIS is Montgomery, my math-test dragon. He is dark red with orange claws and small green spots on his chest.

3. If you make your dragon laugh, it might get smaller. Try telling it jokes.

4. Talk with someone else about your dragon. And remember to get plenty of hugs. Ask for one right now.

This is Montgomery eating my math teacher.

Dragons don't stay forever.
You think they will, but they won't.

You ignore them and you run away from them
and you hide from them and you pretend they're
not dragons and you shout at them and you don't
want to turn out the light and you pay attention
to them and you tell them jokes and you can't think
of anything else and then suddenly...

Hmm... Something feels different.

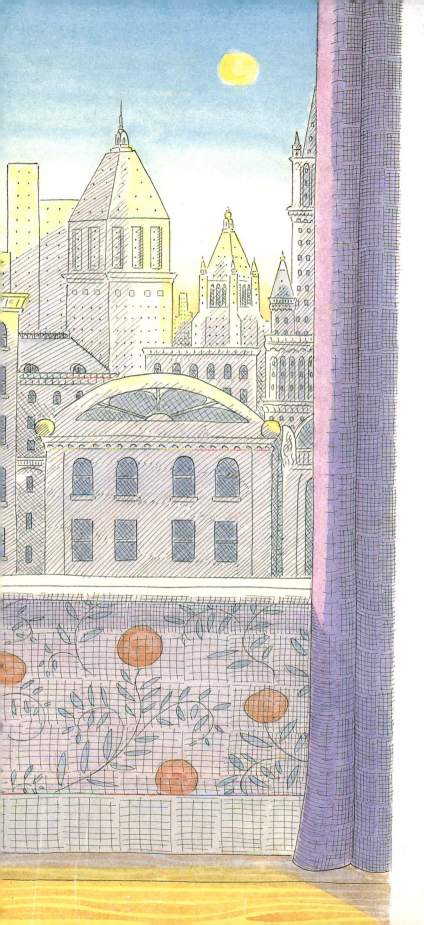

Dragons leave when you least expect them to. You wake up and they're... GONE.

Yours is.
It *really* is.

After all your hard work, your dragon is gone.

Congratulations! Great job!
HURRAY!

(And now you'll know what to do the next time you get dragons.)

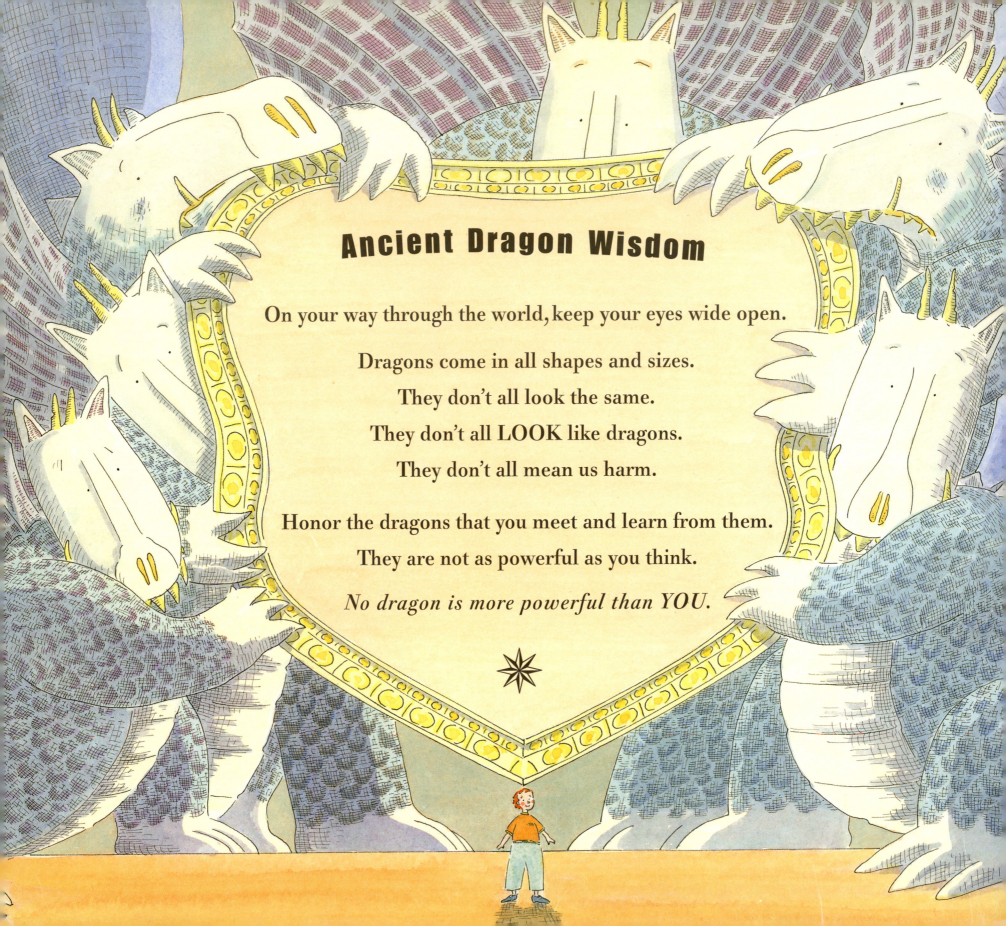

Ancient Dragon Wisdom

On your way through the world, keep your eyes wide open.

Dragons come in all shapes and sizes.

They don't all look the same.

They don't all LOOK like dragons.

They don't all mean us harm.

Honor the dragons that you meet and learn from them.

They are not as powerful as you think.

No dragon is more powerful than YOU.